Crusader A.R.M.s
Vol. I: Assault on Arcadia

Omarr S. Guerrero

DEDICATION

To Jerrin Foote, Cassandra Grandy, Eduardo Huerta, Caesar Mack, Tien Nguyen, and Matt Wills. Without you crazy sons (and daughter) of bitches, I wouldn't be the man I am today. I would be locked in an institution if you guys weren't in my life. Thank you for sparing the wards from my insanity.

CONTENTS

Acknowledgments   i

1   First Strike   1

2   The Beginning   Pg 7

3   Taking Lead   Pg 11

4   Proposed Evolution   Pg 18

5   Wounded Warrior   Pg 24

6   Concern Brothers   Pg 31

7   Tested Bonds   Pg 42

8   Untested Theory   Pg 50

9   Wcapon Packs   Pg 59

10   Night Raid   Pg 64

ACKNOWLEDGMENTS

Thanks to Anna Elizabeth Gamez, Maria Landeros, and Lily Schwambach for beta-reading the story. And special thanks to Eduardo Huerta for pitching ideas to me and for designing the cover.

EPISODE 1: FIRST STRIKE

October 1, 2199

08:12:36

Alarms were blaring throughout the city. "All civilians retreat to the nearest shelter!" said a voice over the PA system. "I repeat: all civilians please retreat to the nearest shelter!" The people stopped what they were doing and rushed to the tunnels that rose from the ground below. Underneath, the people huddled together. Some were crying and some were praying, all while the children eagerly watched the monitors, unaware of the fear the adults were experiencing.

*   *   *

"All pilots report to A.R.M.s bay," said the operator as the alarms continued to blare inside the military headquarters. "Repeat: all pilots report to A.R.M.s bay. Standby for further orders."

Six groups of men and women ran from their rooms, the cafeteria, or wherever they were at, down corridors, and into an elevator that took them down to the hanger. The hanger was five miles in diameter, and housed tens of dozens of military vehicles and ships. Inside were thirty-six 15-meter tall robots. These were the Armored Response Mechs, or A.R.M.s, pilot-operated robots used to fight against planet Earth's greatest threat, yet: savage, insectoid aliens known as the Infestation. The pilots stood in front of a galley in line as General Ian Ulysses Faulkner stepped out of an elevator.

"Listen up, pilots!" he said. "We have a swarm incoming from the east approximately 20 klicks away. Ten Armored Scarabs, each carrying what seems to be type-2 Worker class. They are planning to drop them into the city. Our job is to keep that from happening! Primary defenses are keeping the enemy at bay while you all suit up. We need to prepare a counterattack immediately, got that!?"

"Sir, yes, sir!" shouted the pilots.

"All aerial units are to take out the Scarabs before they reach the city limits. Snipers and other long-range units are to provide support fire near the city's borders. Should the Scarabs get through and drop the workers, the ground forces will be our second line of defense. Ground troops, you will be two to each worker. I don't want any solo acts on this mission! These things are more dangerous than they let on. So, partner up and be careful. Captain Wilson of the Argonauts squad, you are our best flyer, so you will lead the aerial team. Captain Herrera of the Crusaders squad, you are the best sniper, you lead the support team. First Lieutenant Graves of the Crusaders squad, you have the most experience combatting the Infestation in hand-to-hand combat, so you will lead the ground troops. Is all that understood?"

"Sir, yes, sir!"

"Suit up!"

All thirty-six pilots saluted and proceeded to put on their flight suit and climbed into their A.R.M.s. Ephraim Anthony Herrera, captain of the A.R.M.s team Crusaders, walked over to his second in command, Owen Samuel Graves. "You gonna be all right leading, Owen?" he asked, resting his helmet over his shoulder.

"I'll be fine," Owen said, quietly. "Keep an eye on Jensen, yeah?"

"Don't worry, Ghost. I won't let him out of my sight. Plus, I got Chase to back me up, remember?" Ephraim was a 27-year-old Hispanic and stood at five-foot-eight with a medium build. His black hair was in a crew cut style, an example of the perfect soldier.

"Yeah," Owen nodded. He was five-foot-ten, also of Mexican descent with a medium build, and had short dark brown hair that was parted to the side.

Four men walked up to Ephraim and Owen. "Awesome!" said Jensen Mickey Ford, Second Lieutenant and self-proclaimed token black guy of the group. He was 26 and five-foot-eleven. He was lean and bald. "Owen leading the ground forces? That's pretty sweet, dude. Think the others will be able to keep up with you?"

"As long as T.N. can keep the others from getting out of formation, we should be good," Owen said. Science Officer Toshi Gin Nikaido, also referred to as T.N., nodded in agreement.

T.N. was a 27-year-old Vietnamese, older than Ephraim by a month. He had short black hair that he kept neatly trimmed and combed. He was six feet tall with a slender frame that belied his true strength.

"So long as I get to blow shit up," said Sergeant Major Marcus Walker while chewing on a matchstick, "I don't care what I do!" He stood as tall as Owen, but with a slightly thinner build. Mark's sandy blonde hair was short and usually unkempt, and he would always run his fingers through it to get it out of his eyes.

"Just make sure you actually hit something, Mark," Warrant Officer Chase Mercer said, slapping Mark on the back. Chase was the biggest of the six men, although not the tallest, standing at only five-foot-eleven. His muscular build easily made him the tank of team. His straight black hair went down to his shoulders, but Chase usually kept it in a tail similar to the ancient samurais. Mark described Chase as his big ass Filipino friend, whereas Chase described him as the stupid white guy.

"Hey! For your information, Chase, my aim has gotten a lot better!" Mark said.

"Stow it, you two," Ephraim ordered. "Suit up. We need to be ready. And everybody better come back alive. That's an order!"

"Sir!" Jensen, T.N., Chase, and Mark saluted. Owen said nothing. He simply climbed into his A.R.M. and awaited further orders. The others followed suit.

The pilots strapped themselves in as the hatches closed and five monitors lowered into position around the pilot. With the push of a button their A.R.M.s booted up and the monitors displayed the hanger in a crystal-clear image. The pilots settled into their seats and adjusted their grips on the control sticks. The hums from the machines' power cores reverberated from inside their cockpits.

The doors to the hanger, located on the lower area of the city, opened up to a clear blue sky. "Aerial team," said General Faulkner, "you're cleared for take off!"

"Joseph Wilson! Jason, taking off!" One by one, five of the six aerial A.R.M.s, machines capable of transforming from mech mode to fighter jet mode, launched and got into formation.

Jensen was the last to launch. "Jensen Ford! Altair, launching!" The Altair launched from the catapult and took to the skies, joining the others to complete three "V" formations.

"All right, aerial team," Joseph said, "we stay in formation until the bugs are 5 klicks from the border. Once they are, we strike! Our main focus is to make them drop their cargo in the water. Herrera and his team will pick off any stragglers."

"Roger!" responded the aerial team through the radio.

Altair's cameras zoomed in on the incoming enemies. "Sir," Jensen said. "The workers are in their cocoon forms. Shells won't be able to penetrate that kind of armor."

"Shit!" Joseph seethed.

"I got you guys covered," Ephraim radioed.

Back on Arcadia, ten A.R.M.s are connecting generators to a high-caliber sniper rifle on one of the landing strips. Ephraim's A.R.M., the Gryphon, was strapped into the rifle, which was about twice as long as the Gryphon was tall, and was capable of penetrating even the toughest armor. The other nine A.R.M.s readied their weapons; all manner of rifles, rocket launchers, cannons, missiles, and machine guns. Chase's A.R.M., the Minotaur, was a heavy artillery type A.R.M.s. It was bulkier than the rest, but the extra weight gave it better purchase to withstand the recoil of its weapons. The Minotaur held an MRL (Multiple Rocket Launcher) in each hand, and was equipped with missile pods on its legs, waist, and shoulders. On the floor around it was a pair of combat rifles, a laser-guided missile launcher, and Gatling guns for extra firepower.

"Faulkner gave me the green light to use the Eagle Eye," Ephraim informed them. "It should be enough to break through the cocoon."

4

"You know your orders, Herrera?" Joseph asked.

"Just get me a clear shot," Ephraim responded. "Merc, I'm counting on you to watch my back."

"Ain't nothing getting passed me!" Chase said, adjusting the Minotaur's grip on the bazookas.

"Here they come!" shouted Joseph.

The aerial team broke formation as the Armored Scarabs came within range. In their fighter modes, the aerial A.R.M.s had greater speed than the Scarabs, but could only use their GAU-7 machine cannons, which weren't as powerful as their main rifles. The A.R.M.s flew out of the line of fire as the Scarabs released plasma bolts from their mouths. The A.R.M.s and Scarabs were locked in multiple dogfights as Ephraim's team tried to shoot off the silk that held the cocoons to the bugs, but with little success. The bugs were moving way too fast despite the added weight of the cocoons.

Ephraim took his time to line up the shot. He was counting on Jensen to keep the Scarab busy until the opportunity presented itself.

"Just one clear shot," Ephraim whispered to himself. "Just...one..."

Jensen's Altair transformed into its mech mode, kicked the Scarab off balance, transformed back into fighter mode, and flew away.

"Now!" The Gryphon pulled the trigger and fired a concentrated beam of energy that went through both the cocoon and its carrier.

The Scarab, 20-meters long, 10 wide, shrieked as it fell to its death. But the cocoon, at least 30-meters in diameter, did something unthinkable: white bugs, about two meters long, came crawling out and devoured the Scarab almost instantly. The tiny bugs suddenly grew three times in size and sprouted wings. The same thing happened to the other nine cocoons.

"Oh, shit!" Ephraim hissed. "Um, General. I think it's time to send out the ground troops."

"What's going on, Captain?" Faulkner asked. "What happened?"

"The cocoons didn't hold a worker class. They contained larvae that cannibalized their carriers that acted as Miracle-Gro!" Ephraim reported. "I count at least 50 bogeys, sir!"

"Die, you fucking bugs! Die!" Chase roared as his Minotaur

continued its barrage of bullets and missiles.

"Ground forces, you're cleared for launch!" Faulkner ordered.

"Toshi Nikaido! Kirin, launching!"

"Marcus Walker! Agni! It's boom time, baby!"

Owen took a breath and let it out slowly. He struggled to keep his anger reigned in, but overcame it. *'I have to stay focused on the mission,'* he thought to himself. He took another breath, anger finally at bay. "Owen Graves! Fenrir. Commencing destruction!"

EPISODE 2: THE BEGINNING

In the year 2129, in an effort to establish global peace, Earth's nations joined together to construct a new land in the middle of the Pacific Ocean. This new land, called Arcadia, was a symbol of hope for the future. Construction was finally completed on the eve of 2179.

Arcadia was as large as the state of Texas, and was divided into five sectors, all connected by a tram system. The northern sector was dedicated to residential buildings. The western sector was a nature zone, filled with trees, flowers, and a lake. The eastern sector contained industrial mills and factories. The southern sector was where all the recreational facilities were located, such as malls, parks, restaurants, and a zoo. The four outer sectors were all controlled and monitored from the fifth sector, the central hub tower that stood in the middle of the four. This central sector acted as the downtown area of Arcadia, with all sorts of bars and nightclubs surrounding the central tower. Beneath the city was the military headquarters as well as the central power core, which powered the city. The city was kept afloat above the water by a set of four gravity-diffusing generators underneath each sector of the city.

The joined nations, now calling themselves the New Earth Republic Alliance (New E.R.A.), began to bring families into Arcadia to cement the peace. But that peace was short lived, for on February of 2179, disaster struck.

Planet Earth was devastated by a freak meteor storm, demolishing a quarter of the planet. However, that was only the beginning. The meteors brought with them a race of savage, insect-like aliens that ravaged the planet without mercy. The New E.R.A.'s main forces against these creatures were the pilot-operated Armored Response Mechs, commonly referred to as A.R.M.s. Led by General Ian Ulysses Faulkner the A.R.M.s waged an all-out campaign against the aliens known as the Infestation.

For five grueling years, Faulkner and his men fought the Infestation to a standstill. Both sides suffered heavy losses, but it wasn't until the destruction of the queen that the Infestation went into hibernation deep below the planet's surface. New E.R.A. sent out search groups to gather up any survivors of the great cataclysm and escort them to Arcadia.

Though the Infestation were in hibernation, New E.R.A. knew that it was only the calm before the storm. They took the opportunity to train future A.R.M.s pilots at a young age to try and create the perfect soldiers. Over the next 15 years, the E.R.A. trained thirty-six boys and girls as young as 10 years old to pilot the next generation of A.R.M.s. These children were picked based on aptitude scores and psych evaluations, but six of them were handpicked by Faulkner and grouped together. He saw something in these six boys and believed that they would make a great team. Faulkner's beliefs proved fruitful.

Throughout the training process, these six boys grew together and formed a near-perfect unit. Their unit was codenamed Crusaders, and though their reputation was solid, they still fell as the second-best unit in Arcadia. But Faulkner felt that they have yet to reach their full potential.

Ephraim Anthony Herrera was captain of the Crusaders and pilot of the long-range support A.R.M.s Gryphon. Although Ephraim was proficient in hand-to-hand combat, he excelled in marksmanship, mastering any firearm after a single use. Being the best sniper in the E.R.A., Ephraim's Gryphon was often equipped with the high-energy output assault sniper rifle Eagle Eye, a massive sniper rifle powered by several external generators.

Toshi Gin Nikaido, referred to as T.N. by his comrades, was the science officer of the squad and pilot of the close-combat type A.R.M.s Kirin. T.N. was a genius, as well as a master of martial arts, including tae kwon do and judo. He graduated from the New Earth Academy at the top of his class when he was only 7 years old. T.N. led the maintenance teams that oversaw the upgrades, and repairs for all of the A.R.M.s when he wasn't busy leading the science division on research.

Jensen Mickey Ford, second lieutenant and pilot of the transformable aerial type A.R.M.s Altair, was the scout of the group. Able to sneak behind enemy lines without detection for surprise attacks, and get away just as easily using the Altair's Silent Run mode. Jensen was the second best flyer in all the E.R.A., the first being Joseph Wilson, captain of the Argonauts team. But Jensen excelled in a form of dogfighting he called trick flying, performing almost impossible maneuvers that gave him an edge over the other aerial A.R.M.s and the Infestation.

Warrant Officer Chase Julius Mercer was the pilot of the custom heavy artillery A.R.M.s Minotaur. Built with extra armor that concealed missile pods and Gatling guns, the Minotaur was a walking fortress. Although headstrong and, at times, insubordinate, Chase acted as the big brother to the group, willing to jump in the line of fire to protect his comrades. Despite his gung-ho demeanor, Chase has shown a great aptitude for engineering, allowing him to design the custom armor for his machine.

Sergeant Major Marcus Dennis Walker was the certified pyromaniac of the group, specializing in explosives and concussive blasts. His A.R.M. was the close-combat bomber type Agni, which was equipped with a custom grenade launcher designed by T.N. and Chase. Mark, while not formally trained in any martial arts, is an adept street fighter and brawler; capable of taking on ten people at once, a trait he brings to his A.R.M.

Owen Samuel Graves, first lieutenant and second in command of the Crusaders, was a mystery. Aside from the fact that he's fought against the Infestation since age 5 and lost his parents and older brother to them, not much is known about him. He's quiet, cold, and keeps his emotions at bay out of combat, but on the battlefield, he's a force to be reckoned with. Having spent all his life hunting, therefore having the most experience, Owen became the best hunter in the E.R.A., and has used his skills to effectively pilot his A.R.M., the general-purpose type Fenrir.

Despite their drastic differences and reasons for fighting, all six young men have the same goal in mind: eradicate the Infestation and bring humanity back from the brink of extinction. In the year 2199, the Crusader A.R.M.s are the hope for the future...if they can stay alive.

EPISODE 3: TAKING LEAD

October 1, 2199

08:33:55

The ground troops were placed in specific locations around the east district of the city based on T.N.'s plan. Although Owen led them, he relied on T.N.'s tactical genius to bring them to victory.

"Remember the plan, pilots," Owen said. "Wait until they get into the city limits. The defense turrets should draw them to our location."

"Mark, are you sure that this will work?" T.N. asked.

"I know you have your doubts about me, man," Mark replied, "but I've run test after test on this thing and worked seven times out of ten."

"Seven times?" T.N. repeated with a skeptical tone.

"It'll have to do," Owen said. "Beta Team, remain on standby for contingency."

"Sir!" responded the Beta Team over the radio.

A quiet buzzing was the first sign of their arrival as the larvae came flying towards the city at great speed. Ten of the twenty ground troops readied their swords and took aim with their rifles, but made no other moves. Owen's Fenrir held its sword, a katana-like blade, in the air. He kept his focus on the monitors in the cockpit, hands perfectly still on the control sticks. Owen's breathing was steady despite his urge to lash out. The larvae were getting close, yet Owen didn't blink.

When the larvae reached the height of the tallest buildings, Fenrir swung its sword down as Owen shouted, "Now!"

The five A.R.M.s carrying rifles fired at once. The canisters that were launched broke open and formed a single large net, capturing half of the larvae. Mark's Agni was posted on the roof closest to the bugs and shot off an incendiary round from its launcher. The net turned into a green ball of fire, incinerating the captured bugs instantaneously.

"Burn, baby! Burn! Yeah!" Mark roared.

"Cut the shit, Boom!" Owen ordered. "We've still got the other half. Beta Team!"

The rest of the larvae scattered around the city as the other ten A.R.M.s launched from the vertical catapults on top of nearby buildings. They maneuvered themselves and fired their rifles at the bugs, but only managed to clip the wings off of five of them. Beta Team landed on the ground while the twenty uninjured larvae flew down to the injured ones and ate them. The survivors suddenly grew twice in size, making them full-grown Type-2 Worker bugs.

At 12-meters tall, the Workers resembled giant praying mantises, but were bipedal and had four scythe-like arms. The workers were incredibly fast and could shoot plasma bolts from their mouths. Their bladed arms were strong enough to slash through concrete with ease, and their exoskeleton was strong enough to repel machine gun fire.

"Dude! Did you see that?" Mark shouted.

"The method in which they evolve and grow stronger is astounding!" T.N. said, sounding astonished and excited. "I must procure a live specimen."

"It's disgusting," Owen spat. "And I won't make any promises about keeping one alive for you, T.N." Owen saw the Workers getting into formation, one that he instantly recognized. Five of the Workers crouched low on the ground, and five climbed onto the buildings on either side of the first group. The remaining five took to the air and flew around the battleground in a circle, like vultures waiting for a dying animal to finally let go of its last breath. "Ground troops, regroup!" he ordered. "Form a defensive line! Don't let them get any further into the city!"

"Roger!"

"General, we're going to need air support," Owen radioed.

"Aerial team is en route, Lieutenant," Faulkner responded.

"Cap. Merc," Owen called. "You read?"

"Loud and clear, Ghost," responded Ephraim.

"Same," Chase said.

"Larvae have evolved into Type 2 Workers," Owen reported. "They're getting in formation and holding. Air strike is on the way. Cap, you still strapped to the Eagle Eye?"

"Locked and loaded," Ephraim said.

"Get up here and lock onto my position. Fire on my command."

"What? Are you crazy?" Chase exclaimed.

"When did you start giving orders?" Ephraim scoffed sarcastically.

"Just do it!" Owen ordered. "Ground troops, hold position. On my mark, take evasive actions! Aerial team, circle around, transform and fire when we move out of the way!"

"Whoa! Owen is actually giving orders?" Jensen asked.

"Listen to him, troops," Faulkner said.

"Merc, disconnect me from the generators!" Ephraim shouted. "It should have enough power reserved for one shot."

"Gotcha!" Minotaur disconnected the rifle from the generators, and both machines took flight towards the city.

The Workers slowly closed in on the ground A.R.M.s as a faint whining sound buzzed through the radio, causing all the troops to look around frantically. All except Owen. He stayed focused on the enemy in front of him. "Hold your positions!" he ordered.

The whining grew louder every second. The A.R.M.s were getting antsy, but they held. The noise turned into a high-pitch squeal, sending the Workers into a squealing frenzy until something suddenly dropped from the sky. It was a large cocoon, bigger than the ones from before. It cracked open and a 30-meter bug made its way out.

"NOW!"

The ground forces moved out of the way just as Ephraim fired the Eagle Eye at the bug emerging from the cocoon, and the aerial team transformed and rained down hell on the workers. The creatures let loose death squeals as the A.R.M.s continued their assault. Owen and his team got in and took out any who tried to run away. The Fenrir boosted around like a skater, taking off limbs and heads with a savage-like grace. T.N. and Mark managed to capture a wounded bug while the rest of the A.R.M.s made sure the remains of the dead were burned.

The Infestation's attack on Arcadia was over just as quickly as it started. The pilots cheered in triumph for not only did they win the battle, but also very little damage was done to the city and their A.R.M.s. But Owen didn't feel right.

"Well done, pilots!" Faulkner congratulated. "Return to the hanger."

*　　*　　*

At the New E.R.A. headquarters, the staff and military personnel were cheering and shouting in excitement as the pilots returned and congregated in the A.R.M.s bay. The science teams took the captured bug into the labs to study. General Faulkner came into the hanger and everyone stood at attention.

"At ease, soldiers," he said. "That was a fine battle out there today. You all performed admirably."

"Yeah, especially Owen, sir," Jensen said as he smacked Owen's shoulder. Owen didn't react.

"That was excellent leading, First Lieutenant Graves." Faulkner noticed Owen's grim expression. "Are you not happy, Lieutenant?"

"It was too easy," Owen said. "This battle was too easily won."

"You call that easy?" said another pilot.

"This was merely a test to gauge our strength, General," Owen continued, ignoring the other pilot.

"You're sure of this?" Faulkner asked. Owen nodded. "What do you suggest?"

"Put an A.R.M.s team on sentry duty, rotating teams for the next couple of days, keep the city on high alert, keep the auto-turrets online, and be ready for a night raid. I volunteer for first watch, sir."

Faulkner saw it in Owen's eyes. He'd seen this method before. Owen always had a knack for predicting the Infestation's moves. Perhaps it was a result of how he grew up.

"No," Faulkner said, shaking his head. "You get some rest. Centurion squad, report back in 2300 hours for first watch. Everyone else get some rest.

"But, sir," Owen pleaded.

"That was a direct order, Lieutenant." Owen said nothing. Faulkner then said, "Besides, you have an appointment later today, right? You don't want to keep her waiting."

"Yes, sir," Owen said begrudgingly. Owen saluted the general and walked out of the hanger. He went down the corridor that led to his quarters where the rest of his team caught up with him. They entered the barracks and gathered around Owen.

"Way to go, Owen!" Jensen cheered, hanging off of Owen. "You're the man of the hour!"

"With more plans like those," said Mark, plopping himself down on one of the bunks in the room, "we'll finish off the Infestation in no time!"

"It was T.N.'s plan," Owen said.

"Yes, but it was your leadership skills that executed the plan perfectly," T.N. responded. "You should be proud of that."

"Yeah," Chase agreed. "You could give Ephraim a run for captain."

Ephraim shrugged his shoulders. "I wouldn't mind taking a vacation."

"I don't want to be captain," Owen said, shrugging Jensen off his back. "I just want to put an end to this. Now if you'll excuse me, I'm late for an appointment."

"Gonna see that therapist of yours, huh, Owen?" Jensen asked.

"Man, she is smoking!" Chase exclaimed.

"Yeah, dude," Mark chimed in. "When are you going to seal the deal with her?"

Owen shot Mark a glare. "If you like her so much, you ask her out. I'm only seeing her as a condition to be an A.R.M.s pilot."

"Don't mind if I do," Mark said and hopped off the bed to leave, but was pulled back by Ephraim.

"Get back here, Mark!" Ephraim smacked him upside the head and said, "We need to use this time wisely. Owen's never wrong when it comes to the bugs. They'll be back with a stronger force. We need to be prepped and rested when that happens. Mark, I need you to make more of those nets."

"Got it," Mark saluted.

"T.N.," Ephraim continued, "I believe you have a specimen you are eager to examine."

"Indeed I do," T.N. said, grabbing his lab coat from the closet and putting it on.

"Chase, Jensen, get some R&R."

"Cool," Jensen chirped, jumping onto one of the top bunks.

"Awesome," said Chase.

"As for me, I've got somebody waiting for me."

"Aww!!!" Jensen, Chase, and Mark teased.

"Send her my greetings," T.N. said, and walked out of the room.

Ephraim nodded. Owen left the room without saying a word.

"Think he'll ever fully open up?" Jensen asked.

"Not while the Infestation is still around," Ephraim said. "Just give him till then. He'll come around."

EPISODE 4: PROPOSED EVOLUTION

11:09:44

Down in the lab a team of scientists monitored the captured bug as it continued its attempts to break free. One scientist took x-rays while another took photographs. Others were taking notes on its movements and body readings. One recorded its cries while another filmed the entire process.

T.N. walked in, lab coat over his uniform. "What do you have for me?" he asked.

"Dr. Nikaido," said one of the scientists, rushing over to T.N. and handing him an electronic tablet. "This creature is incredible! Its metabolism is constantly adjusting itself, rebuilding and regenerating dead cells, allowing it to heal at an exponential rate. It also secretes a fluid in high temperatures, almost as if it is sweating and keeping the body cool. This fluid also acts as a deterrent to predators. Who knows what else it can be used for?"

"A bug that sweats?" T.N. pondered. "Why would the Infestation worry about predators? They are the dominant species on the planet."

"Maybe they had predators back on their planet," suggested the scientist.

"Dr. Nikaido!" another scientist shouted as she came running from one of the cubicles. "Dr. Nikaido!"

"What is it, Laura?" he asked.

"Something you should see," she said in between breaths, handing him a folder.

T.N. took the folder and opened it up. Looking through the x-rays of the Worker, T.N. almost dropped the folder. He looked through them again, eyes wide, trying to understand what he was seeing. "How can this be? This bug has both an exoskeleton and an endoskeleton!"

"How is that possible?" the first scientist asked as the others looked with surprise.

"That's what we're going to find out."

*　　*　　*

15:40:00

T.N. and his team continued studying the Worker's behavior. After hours of observations, the scientists discovered that the fluid it secreted produced a rancid smell that is assumed to ward off any would-be attackers. The plasma bolts the bug fired was a mix of liquid silk and digestive juices. Its mandibles were strong enough to crush concrete, but have trouble with steel and other strong metals.

T.N. sat at his desk and turned on his computer. *This creature has all the basic functions of a praying mantis proportionate to its size,* T.N. thought to himself. *But the existence of the endoskeleton has yet to be explained.* He continued to type his findings into the computer. *The scans of its internals show that the bug's organs are placed in a similar manner to that of a human, with the exception of the extra ligaments for the wings and arms. This is bizarre beyond all accounts.*

T.N. leaned back in his chair, staring up at the metal ceiling. *Why would the Infestation come to Earth?* he pondered. *Two decades and we're still nowhere close to understanding their motives. I thought obtaining another live specimen would provide us with some answers, but instead we get more questions.*

T.N. rubbed his head to try and focus on the information.

"Argh!" he grunted as he slammed his hand on the desk in frustration. The other scientists stared at him. "I'm okay," T.N. assured them. "I'm going to get some air. Send any new data you discover to my terminal."

As the elevator climbed from the underground up to the surface, T.N. stood and mulled over what he had discovered. *Those x-rays. They remind me of an experiment I assisted with back in my days at the academy. Splicing human DNA with that of insects. But that's not possible. The Infestation are aliens, aren't they?*

The elevator stopped and its doors opened, but T.N. made no attempts to leave. He pulled out his terminal, a small computer that produced a holographic display and keyboard, and started browsing through his files and research. He stopped at a photo of himself during his graduation from the New Earth Academy when he was 7. Next to him in the photo was an older man, a man whom T.N. held the utmost respect for. His name was Hubert Kirchner. He was the head of the N.E.A. and was billed as the top scientist for human development.

"Professor Kirchner," T.N. mutter to himself. "Has someone taken your noble ideals and twisted them into these abominations?"

*　　*　　*

New Earth Academy – January, 20 years ago

"Mankind, as a species, has reached the pinnacle of its evolutionary tract," Professor Hubert Kirchner announced to the auditorium filled with all of the top scientists of their respective fields. "Rather than evolving into higher beings, humanity will devolve back into the Neanderthals in the generations to come."

Professor Kirchner paused as the room filled with his colleagues talked amongst themselves, taking his words into consideration.

"If we are to guide humanity towards the stars," Kirchner continued, "then we must take the necessary steps to better mankind and evolve."

"What are you trying to say, Kirchner?" asked one of his colleagues. "Are you implying that we force evolution on humanity?"

"No, no. Not force it," Kirchner reassured him. "I am proposing that we coax and lead it in the right direction. Mr. Nikaido, if you please." A young Toshi Nikaido stood up from his seat behind the professor and turned on a holographic projector that displayed an animated model of a man. "Thank you. Now as we all know, the bones in a person's body will become brittle in extended periods of zero gravity, and artificial gravity can only do so much to alleviate the problem. But what if we modified our bone structure to be able to withstand long periods of zero gravity?"

"Are you suggesting that we manipulate our genes to become stronger?" a fellow scientist asked with a skeptical tone.

"Manipulate is such an ugly word," Kirchner said. "I prefer enhance. I have developed a formula that will enhance not only the strength and flexibility of our bones, but also our physical strength, healing capabilities, reflexes, and endurance in higher gravity. However, I've run into a slight complication."

"What complication?"

"When I tested the formula on rats, their metabolism increased to accommodate the increased healing, but that effectively decreased their lifespan."

"I'm curious, Kirchner," said a scientist by the name of William Matthias, the head of the genetics department. "What did you use as the foundation for your formula?"

"Insect biology," Kirchner answered.

"Interesting," Matthias mused. "It just so happens that my department has been developing a new base protein that can fix your metabolic problem, Hubert. Think of it like this: if we combine both our projects together, we can use it in military applications. A new string of super soldiers for the new generation."

The auditorium was abuzz with murmurs as the scientists talked amongst themselves, debating on the idea of weaponizing this formula.

"Absolutely not!" boomed a young voice from the stage. Everyone turned and saw Toshi walk up to the podium, a stern look on his face. Only 7 years old and already he held such prestige in the scientific community. "Professor Kirchner's formula will not become a product of war! The planet is at peace and all disputes have been settled. What reason is there to create super soldiers?"

Kirchner smiled at his pupil. Toshi had learned so much in such a short amount of time. He had shared Kirchner's ideals on human development, and wished to see humanity travel the stars, but Matthias would always step in and try to use Toshi for his own ends. Matthias was more of a warmonger than a scientist, and would use every method he knew to try and corrupt the young genius. However, Toshi always stood firm in his beliefs. He never wavered.

Until Matthias finally broke him…

*   *   *

Present day

15:55:12

"All pilots to A.R.M.s bay! Repeat: all pilots to A.R.M.s bay!"

The announcement over the loudspeakers roused T.N. from his thoughts. He looked around, slightly confused, and saw other pilots scrambling toward other open elevators. "Are we being attacked?" he asked one of them who entered his elevator, a female by the name of Rachel Stewart, major of the Amazon A.R.M.s team.

"I don't know, sir," Rachel responded. "But it's been announced as a code blue."

"A distress signal? From where?"

The doors closed as the last of the pilots got in, and the elevator went down. "The White House."

EPISODE 5: WOUNDED WARRIOR

15:10:26

Owen sat in the big chair across from the desk as he waited for his therapist to arrive. He hated coming to these sessions, but it was the only thing General Faulkner asked of Owen in order to pilot an A.R.M. Owen looked at the clock on the wall behind him. "She's late," he muttered and let out a sigh.

The office was basic. It had sky blue walls, a bookshelf on one wall, and a plant across from it. The wall behind the desk held frames of diplomas and a couple of photos of a family. Owen drummed his fingers on his lap and felt something in his pocket, and pulled it out. It was an old wooden flute, the last reminder he had of his family. It was made from black wood and had silver circles surrounding the keyholes. Owen's father got it on a trip to Ireland where he first met his mother. It was then given to Francis, Owen's older brother, on his first camping trip. Francis, then, left it for Owen before he died.

Owen put the instrument to his lips and started to play. The tune came out slow and somber, every note hanging in the air. He switched to a lighter, faster tune, and continued playing, switching between the two tempos. The door behind him suddenly opened and Owen immediately stopped playing.

"It's about time you played again," said a woman in a blue business outfit. She had fair skin and her dark hair was put up in a bun. "That was beautiful."

"You're late, Dr. Noble."

"I was waiting outside the door," she said. "I had hoped you would play again if I made you wait long enough. And look. You did." She smiled at Owen, making her green eyes sparkle. Owen did nothing. "So, Owen, how are we today?"

"The same, Dr. Noble."

"Seriously, Owen?" she sighed, shaking her head. "I've repeatedly asked you to call you me Christine. Is that so hard?"

"Calling you by your first name acknowledges a relationship beyond the professional level," Owen said, void of emotion. "I don't have time for such distractions."

"Yet, *Owen*," Christine said, emphasizing his name, "you called your teammates by their nicknames today, didn't you?"

Owen turned to her, eyes wide with surprise, and then looked away in embarrassment. "You--you heard that?" Christine smiled again. "I--I was caught in the heat of the moment," he stammered. "That was it."

Christine sat on the edge of her desk, facing Owen. "I bet you were," she teased. "Considering it was your first time leading in battle."

"How--"

"Did I know?" she finished for him. "I was in the command center during the attack. Faulkner asked me to observe. I must say, Owen, you are one hell of a leader. It's a natural fit for you."

"I don't want to lead. I just—"

"I know. I know. You just want to put an end to the Infestation." Christine placed her hand on Owen's and said, "There must be something else you want to do besides fight." She saw a faint glimmer in his eyes before he turned away. "Owen, when are you going to open up? When are you going to let others in?"

"I don't want to open up. I just want to complete my mission."

Christine knelt in front of Owen and looked deep into his dark eyes. He looked back and saw something in her eyes. Was it sadness? Concern? Or something else? They stayed like that for a few moments, her hand still on his. Owen felt his heart beat faster the longer they gazed at each other. And then he felt something else.

"Chris, I--I can't," he spoke softly. "I just…"

"You don't have to be afraid to show your emotions, Owen," Christine said just as softly. "You don't have to be afraid, not with me. You're not alone anymore."

Owen hesitated for a moment, heart beating faster. He moved his hand away from hers, but it was much slower than he had intended.

Christine smiled, knowing that Owen did want to open up to her, but he couldn't figure out how. "Could you play your flute for me, Owen?" she asked. "Just once?"

Owen gave her the briefest of smiles and put the instrument to his lips again. He closed his eyes and started to play. The notes came out slow, resonating in the air as they rose. The tune had a sad feeling to it, filled with Owen's pain and anguish, but as he played, the music changed to a more upbeat pace. Christine watched as Owen played, a pleased smile spreading across her face.

The beeping from Owen's terminal cut short the music, killing the moment between the two. "Damn," Owen muttered with a frown, much to Christine's surprise. He grabbed the terminal from its holster on his belt and activated the display. "It's a message from the general."

"Another attack?"

"A distress signal. Chris, I've got to—"

"I know, Owen. Promise me you won't do anything reckless."

Owen got up from the chair and said, "I'll be careful," before heading to the door. He opened it, but he didn't leave just yet. "You play the violin, right, Dr. Noble?"

Christine stood up with a puzzled look on her face. "I'm a little rusty, but yeah. Why?"

"Maybe," he hesitated, not turning to face her. "Maybe we could--we could play together." Owen left the office before she could answer.

"Sure, Owen," Christine smiled as she watched him leave for his next mission. "We can play together."

* * *

15:45:33

Mark sat on a workbench in the armory alone, tying lengths of detonation cord into braids. It took him two days to make the incendiary nets used in the battle that morning, and Mark regretted not letting Jensen and Chase help him. Despite his carefree attitude and lack of tact, however, Mark was a genius when it came to explosives, and he would rather take longer to make sure everything was done right than risk failure.

His fingers nimbly weaved the cords. The braids were even and tight. It was just as his father taught him during their time together. Malcolm Walker, his two sons, and daughter were some of the few survivors in their neighborhood. Malcolm had gathered whomever he could find and brought them all together. He led them to a small part of the city that was still relatively intact. There they pooled their talents together in order to survive.

Mark remembered his father fondly. He remembered how to tie nets together, build traps and pitfalls. But one lesson Malcolm taught that stuck with Mark, and saved his life many times over, was how to build all manner of explosives. Jensen would often ask him if he could make a bomb out of bubblegum, a bottle cap, and paperclip. His friend and teammate's antics always brought a smile on Mark's face.

The alarms went off, signaling all pilots to head to the command center. Mark's terminal went off at the same time, providing further information on the situation. "A code blue? From the White House?" Mark closed his terminal and prepared to leave, but stopped to look at the picture of him and his family.

"I'll get them for you, Dad," Mark said, picking up the photo. "I'll fight to make sure Peter and Natalie, as well all of those you saved, will have a bright future. I promise." He put it down on the table and left the armory toward the command center.

*   *   *

15:40:51

Jensen and Chase sat at their usual table in Gordon's Diner. The diner was located near an elevator that led to the A.R.M.s hanger. The two sat in a big booth next to a window. The booth could hold the team comfortably. Chase was eating an omelet with a large side of rice while Jensen ate a slice of peach cobbler. Chase would always grow a huge appetite after a battle, and the others would frequent the diner after a battle as well.

Jensen hadn't touched his pie in a while. He sat in his seat, watching the people go about their lives as if nothing had happened. *How nice to live a life without risk,* he thought to himself. Jensen let out a sigh and took a sip of his coffee.

"Everything okay, Moogz?" Chase asked through a mouthful of rice.

"Ever wonder why we fight?"

"You mean besides protecting our homes and family?"

"Yeah, but I mean in general. Human history is full of fighting. And for what? For glory? For land? Power?" Jensen shook his head. "I don't know, man. Maybe I'm just being stupid."

Chase swallowed the rice he had in his mouth and drank some of his water. "It's questions like those that allow us to keep our humanity," he finally said. "I enjoy the action and the weapons I get to use. But if I had a choice, I wouldn't fight. I would rather use my know-how to go to school and get a job to support my brothers and sister."

"See? You have a reason to fight, though," Jensen said. "I feel out of place in the team."

"I'm not good at this whole philosophical debate about human actions, but I know one thing. It was something that Ephraim told us remember? If you have the ability to make a difference, if you have the power to protect, then you have an obligation to put those abilities to good use. Jensen, just because you haven't lost anybody doesn't mean you shouldn't fight. In fact, you have more reason to fight than any of us."

"I do?" Jensen asked, puzzled by Chase's deep response.

Chase nodded. "You have to protect your folks from the bad in this world. Be it the Infestation or just some douche trying to start something. I fight to protect my siblings. Mark fights to protect his.

Ephraim fights to protect Gwen. T.N. fights for knowledge. And Owen fights for survival."

"Cap always did say something about it being better to die on your feet than on your knees," Jensen remembered.

"Yeah, but Ephraim is also a boy scout. He'll do or say anything to make him sound more patriotic. But he also did say that everyone has a reason to fight, remember? Even the civilians have a reason to fight."

Jensen smiled. "Yeah, I remember. We fight to survive."

Just then, their terminals started to beep. They grabbed them from their holsters and activated the screens. "A code blue?" Chase muttered.

"At the White House? What the hell? Didn't that place get trashed during the storm?" Jensen asked.

"Only one way to find out. Let's go!"

Jensen and Chase left money on the table and rushed out of the diner to HQ.

EPISODE 6: CONCERNED BROTHERS

October 1, 2199

16:04:02

The 36 A.R.M.s pilots gathered in the command center where a large screen displayed a map of the former United States, or rather what was left of it. A red light was blinking on the Washington D.C. area. Some of the pilots were getting antsy while they waited for General Faulkner to arrive.

"How is this possible?" Chase asked his teammates. "Wasn't the White House destroyed during the storm?"

"I, too, find this rather peculiar," T.N. agreed.

"No one could have survived that much destruction," Jensen chimed in.

"Quiet," Ephraim ordered.

The doors to the command center opened up and Faulkner walked in. "At ease, soldiers," he commanded. "As you can tell, we are receiving a distress signal from the ruins of the White House. How is this possible, you're all wondering. Communications team has ruled out the possibilities of survivors and passed it off as a glitch in the circuitry. However, I am not one to ignore distress signals, and neither is the Faculty. So, I'll be dispatching an A.R.M.s team to the area to check it out."

"Sir," Ephraim stepped up. "The Crusaders will volunteer for this mission."

"I appreciate it, Captain Herrera, but I have already decided on sending the Titans out. I need you and Science Officer Nikaido for another mission."

"Sir!" Ephraim saluted and stepped back in line.

"Even though the team has already been chosen, you all need to know this." Faulkner clicked a button on the display's controller and the map changed to a video feed from an A.R.M.s factory. "Our partners at Camelot have been working diligently on developing new armaments specifically tailored to each pilot. The first series of these weapons have just been finished. They are for the Argonauts, Crusaders, and Centurions teams."

The command center was filled with a mix of cheers and groans. Mark, Jensen, and Chase gave each other a high-five, followed by a little victory dance.

Faulkner cleared his throat and said, "Captain Herrera, your team's mission is to escort the carrier containing the weapons back to HQ. That way Science Officer Nikaido can make any necessary adjustments and equip your A.R.M.s during flight."

"Yes, sir!" the Crusaders saluted.

"Marauders, you will be on guard duty around Arcadia," Faulkner continued with his orders. "The rest of you, tune up your machines, get in some practice, get some rest; do whatever you need to do to be at top condition. We are still expecting a follow-up attack. Be ready for anything. Dismissed!"

"Sir, yes sir!" saluted the pilots.

The six teams left the command center and went down to the A.R.M.s bay to prep their machines. The Titans were first to launch to carry out their search mission. The Marauders launched next to begin their duty around the city.

The Crusaders were in the locker rooms, suiting up for departure. Their pilot suits were black, but had stripes from the sides of the torso, down to the knees. Similar stripes went down from the shoulders to the elbows. Each pilot had his own color. Ephraim's stripes were red. Owen had navy blue stripes. Jensen's were purple. Chase had orange. Mark's were green, and T.N.'s were gray.

"T.N.," Ephraim called out after shutting his locker. "Come on. Gives us the skinny on these new weapons."

"Can't," T.N. smirked. "It's classified."

"Come on, T.," Jensen pleaded. "Give your buddies a little somethin'."

"We're getting more bang for our buck, right?" Mark asked.

"Mark, if you get any more explosives," Chase said, "you'll end up finishing off the human race before the bugs do."

"Oooh! What is it?" Mark asked.

"It's a surprise," T.N. said. "One that you will all enjoy."

"I hate surprises," Ephraim groaned.

"Yeah," said Jensen. "Remember that time I put that rubber spider in your bed on your birthday while you were sleeping, Cap?"

"Ugh!" Ephraim shuddered. "I can't believe Gwen helped you with that! I hate spiders!"

"Well, it was actually her idea." Jensen and the others laughed as Ephraim shuddered in disgust again.

Owen shut the door to his locker, not having said a single word since the briefing, but his teammates had noticed something peculiar about him. Mark went up to Owen and scrutinized the details of his face. Owen's dark eyes held a slight gleam in them and his usual frown was turned into a small smile. Mark continued to examine him.

"Can I help you?" Owen asked, slightly annoyed.

"Hey, guys!" Mark called out. "Owen got laid!"

"WHAT!?" shouted the others, rushing towards Owen's side.

"Tell us all about it!" Jensen said with glee.

"There's nothing to tell," Owen said. "We just talked."

"Is that what they're calling it these days?" Ephraim chided.

Chase smiled. "Ha! It's about damn time you made your move!"

"Piss off!" Owen snapped, shoving his way through the others.

Ephraim grabbed Owen's shoulder. "Dude, come on. Chill. We're just trying to have fun. We're family, man. Lighten up. Make a joke. Smile, baby!"

That slight glimmer in Owen's eyes was gone, replaced with the coldness they usually held. He shrugged off his captain's hand and walked away from the team to his machine. "My family's dead," they heard him say, cold and bitter.

"That was harsh," Jensen said.

"Sorry, Cap," said Mark. "Didn't mean to piss him off."

"It's okay, Boom. Let's just get our machines onboard the carrier and head out."

* * *

17:33:50

The team had been in the air for an hour already, but they had another four to go. Ephraim sat in the copilot's seat of the A.R.M.s transport carrier named Fat Boy. The transport's pilot was Casey Gardner. She was the Crusaders' usual pilot, and had gained a sort of sister-like relationship with the guys. She wore her trademark brown bomber hat and jacket, vintage red Doc Marten's boots with black jeans and tank top. Her shoulder length brown hair was tied in pigtails.

"So do you guys expect to see any action in this mission?" Casey asked.

"I hope not," Ephraim answered. "But T.N. says that we should be ready for any possible danger."

"Understandable, but did you have to bring all six of your A.R.M.s?" Casey complained. "They're making the Fat Boy's ass even fatter!"

Ephraim chuckled. "Couldn't be helped. Those were our orders. Faulkner wants us equipped and ready by the time we return to Arcadia."

"And add more weight to my poor baby? No way!"

"He'll be fine, Case. Besides, this thing was made to easily carry ten units. So quit your moaning."

"Fine, but if you scratch the paint, I'm tearing you a new asshole!"

"Geez, you're moody today."

In the cargo hold, Mark, Jensen, Chase, and T.N. were sitting on the floor, playing cards. Mark's pile of chips was stacked high. Jensen and Chase were down to about half their pile. T.N.'s pile was almost gone, yet his calm demeanor puzzled the others.

"Five bucks says that T.N. is playing Mark," Jensen whispered to Chase.

"Ten," he whispered back.

Mark shuffled the deck several times before dealing out the

cards. The four picked up their cards and eyed each other. Mark tried his best to hide his grin, but the others saw it clearly. He pushed in his entire stack of chips and boldly said, "All in!"

Jensen and Chase looked from Mark, to each other, and then to T.N. His face had not twitched when he shoved the remainder of his chips into the pile. Chase and Jensen looked at each other again. "Fuck it!" they both blurted as they dropped their cards to the floor.

"Ready to call it quits, T.N.?" Mark boasted.

"Funny. I was going to ask you the same thing."

Mark slapped his cards down, shouting, "Full House, baby! Read 'em and weep!"

"Oh," T.N. uttered with what sounded like concern. "My, that is a tough hand to beat." Jensen and Chase were holding each other in mock fear as T.N. continued. "But I believe my friends have something to say about that. Have you met them?" T.N. placed his cards down one-by-one while calling out their names. "Ten. Jack. Queen. King." He stopped to savor the look on Mark's face before placing the final card down. "Ace."

"Royal Flush, mother fucker!" Chase jumped and hollered.

"God dammit!" Mark cried.

"Better luck next time, bro," Jensen said, patting Mark on the shoulder. "Now, who wants to play Go Fish?"

"Why don't you ask Owen if he wants to play?" T.N. suggested. "I would do it myself, but I'm far too busy counting my winnings."

"Jerk," Mark muttered.

"He still hasn't come out of Fenrir?" Jensen asked. "It's almost been two hours!"

"His lone wolf act is starting to get really annoying," Chase said.

"Can't be helped," T.N. stated. "We can't force him to open up. That's something he alone can do."

"But we've been together for 15 years," Jensen said. "Shouldn't that be enough time to get comfortable around us?"

"Maybe that's just it," T.N. suggested. "Maybe he doesn't want to get comfortable around us. He may not want to open up. After all, this is a battlefield. Any one of us could die at any time. That may be how he copes with the pain; by distancing away from us, he won't have to feel."

"But that's cold," Mark said. "We'd be pissed if he were to die. I mean, come on! We're bros!"

"He doesn't see it that way," Jensen put in, recalling Owen's words back at the base. "The guy literally has no one. My family and I were already on Arcadia before the meteors hit, same as Toshi. Mark, you still have your brother and sister, along with the survivors you and your pops saved before being brought to the city. Chase has his two brothers and sister. And Cap's got Gwen. If you think about it, Owen is more alone than any one of us could ever know."

Inside Fenrir's cockpit, Owen watched his teammates play cards on the main monitors. When the game was over, he heard them talk about him. He heard the concern in their words, but there was nothing he could do about it. Not right now, anyway.

You don't have to be afraid to show your emotions. You're not alone anymore. Christine's words echoed in Owen's mind *You don't have to be afraid with me.*

"I am alone," he spoke aloud. "But I am not afraid. I just—I just…" Owen choked on his words as those long-buried emotions slowly crept up. He shut his eyes tight, forcing the emotions back in their cages, refusing to let even a single tear fall. "No! Now is not the time. I have to stay focused." Owen took several deep breaths to regain his composure. He grabbed his flute from his backpack and said to himself, "This is the least I can do for them." He brought the wooden instrument to his lips and started to play.

The music came out slow, but it had a joyous sound to it. The notes echoed throughout the ship, carrying with it a flighty, almost heroic, melody.

"What is that?" Mark asked, searching for the source of the music.

"It's Owen," T.N. said, sitting against Kirin's leg and enjoying the music.

"I didn't know he could play the flute," Jensen said.

"Not surprising," T.N. said. "Just sit back and enjoy. Who knows when he'll decide to play again."

The four men sat back and listened to Owen's song, enjoying the melody. Back in the ship's cockpit, Casey was bobbing her head while Ephraim reviewed his mission notes on his terminal.

"Seems like you're breaking through to Owen," Casey said.

"Actually, I think it might be his therapist who's getting through to him."

"That Christine chick? God, she's gorgeous! If I went that way, I'd ravage her!" Casey paused to think for a second. "Fuck it. I'll ravage her even if I don't go that way!"

Ephraim looked over to Casey and rolled his eyes. After a minute, he took a deep breath and let out a relaxed sigh. "Yeah, I just hope Dr. Noble will be able to pull it off."

"It seems like she genuinely likes him."

"Yeah," Ephraim nodded his head in agreement. "Although he won't admit it, but Owen likes her, too."

"Speaking of which, how's Gwen?"

Ephraim smiled at the thought of his fiancé. They had been best friends since they were kids, but after the meteors hit, they both lost everything. They became inseparable since. After he finished his A.R.M.s training, Ephraim proposed to Gwen. "She's great. She should be with her friends looking for a dress."

"So, you've settled on a date?"

"Well, no, but it's a good idea that we get what we need first to have less to worry about. Plus, this gives her plenty of time to try out all the dresses she wants."

"You're such a sweetheart, Cap."

"I am, aren't I? What about you and Noah? Got plans for the future?"

"Oh, we've got plans," Casey smiled. "But first we're gonna get a puppy!"

"We're thinking about getting one, too! Ooh! Our puppies can be best buddies and have play dates!"

"Yay!" Casey cheered.

Their laughter was abruptly cut when an alarm on her dashboard went off.

"What the?" Ephraim looked at Casey.

"Proximity sensors are picking up something closing in fast!" she reported.

A jolt rocked the ship off balance. Casey disabled the autopilot and took over the controls to level the ship.

"What the hell was that?" Ephraim asked.

"I don't know," Casey replied. "But we've lost an engine!"

The ship took another hit. "Hold on, baby," Casey cried.

"I'm activating the auto turrets!" Ephraim shouted.

"Open the hatch," Owen's voice buzzed through the intercom.

"Owen, stay on the ship. That's an order!" Ephraim commanded. "Jensen, get out and check what's attacking. While he does that, the rest of you suit up and prepare for evac!"

"Fuck you and your orders!" Owen spat. "Fat Boy needs to lose some weight in order to stay aloft. I'm going, too."

"Fenrir isn't suited for aerial combat—"

"Just do it!" Owen barked, almost drowning out the alarms.

Ephraim nodded reluctantly to Casey, who proceeded to pull the lever that controlled the rear loading doors. "Jensen, keep an eye on him."

"Roger!"

The wind was rushing in as Fenrir moved to the opened doors, armed with its sword, a high-powered rifle, and shield. Altair moved up behind Fenrir equipped with an assault rifle and machine gun. T.N., Mark, and Chase boarded their A.R.M.s right after.

"You sure you want to do this, Ghost?" Jensen asked.

Fenrir dropped out of the ship, its grey and navy blue paint blending in with the night sky. The thrusters on its back and legs kept the unit steady in the air, but its flight time was limited. Its head scanned the surrounding area, searching for any signs of the attackers, when the proximity sensors went off. Six dragonfly-types–Drakes–the size of a fighter jet, sped towards Fenrir, blasting bolts of plasma the closer they got.

Fenrir evaded two of the projectiles, but its maneuverability in midair paled in comparison to its ground agility. Owen raised the shield, blocking three of the attacks, but the last one hit Fenrir's right leg.

"Shit!" Owen hissed, firing the rifle in three-burst shots.

The Drakes scattered and tried to surround Fenrir, but a pair of missiles struck one of the bugs, blowing it up. Altair swooped down and around in its fighter mode, breaking up the enemy's formation.

"Yee-haw!" Jensen drawled. "Let's round up them varmints and put an end to this here battle quick-like!"

"No shit," Owen replied, ignoring Jensen's Western accent and focused on keeping Fenrir in the air.

The Drakes swarmed in, trying to surround the two machines

while charging up their blasts, but Fenrir charged one at full speed, bashing the shield in its face. Owen stabbed the barrel to the rifle in the bug's compound eye and opened fire, blasting goo and other wet matter all over Fenrir. The bug shrieked in pain, causing the other four to charge in towards Fenrir. Altair transformed to its mech mode and released a barrage of bullets from the machine gun and rifle, taking out two more before they could overwhelm Owen. It transformed back to fighter mode and allowed Fenrir to land on top of it.

Riding Altair like a surfboard, Fenrir swooped around and outmaneuvered the bugs, evading a volley of bolts. Owen lined up the rifle's sights on one of them while Jensen locked a missile on to the other. With a squeeze of the trigger, both A.R.M.s fired their weapons and blasted the two remaining Drakes into goo.

"That's the last of them," Jensen radioed. "Let's head back to Fat Boy. Ghost? Ghost, you okay up there?" No response. "Hey, Owen!"

"Evasive maneuvers!" Owen shouted.

Fenrir jumped off the Altair and both evaded a large sphere of plasma, but the projectile flew past them and blew a hole in the aft of their transport. Through the thick mist came six Goliath-class hornets escorting a Goliath-class horned beetle. Fenrir and Altair hovered in the air, waiting for the next attack, as Fat Boy went down.

EPISODE 7: TESTED BONDS

18:10:00

The alarms continued to blare frantically as Fat Boy spun out of control. Kirin, Agni, and Minotaur jumped out of the hatch and fell fast towards the vast ocean below. The three pilots released the parachutes to their machines and gained control of their descent, guiding the A.R.M.s to a strip of nearby islands.

"Casey, we have to get out of here!" Ephraim urged.

"I am not leaving my ship!" Casey shouted back. "Get into your machine! Now!"

"Fuck this captain-going-down-with-the-ship crap! Let's go!" Ephraim grabbed Casey's arm and pulled her away from the ship's controls. "Come on, you stubborn bitch!"

"No!" she screamed as she fought against Ephraim's grip.

A loud clang echoed from below and Fat Boy suddenly leveled itself. There was a loud metallic groan as something pushed up against the ship. "I can't hold it for long, Cap!" Jensen radioed. "Hurry up and get your asses out of there!"

"Thanks, Moogz!" Ephraim said. "Sorry, Case, but I've got no choice." He grabbed Casey and lifted her up in a fireman's carry.

"What? No! Let me go! I am not leaving my baby!"

Ephraim sprinted from the cockpit to the cargo hold, bracing himself against Casey's flailing. There, Gryphon was in a kneeling position, hatch open, waiting for its pilot to return. Ephraim carried her up to the hatch and tossed her in, jumping in right after. The systems booted up as the hatch closed and Ephraim strapped himself in. Armed with a sniper rifle, heavy assault rifle, dual pistols, and a missile pod on its left leg, Gryphon made its way to the cargo doors and leapt out of the ship. The thrusters activated, keeping the machine in the air.

Altair let go of Fat Boy and watched it crash onto the beach. Altair transformed into its fighter mode and flew towards Gryphon, allowing it to land on top.

"Rest in peace, Fat Boy," Casey mourned, tears falling down her cheeks.

"Where's Ghost?" Ephraim asked.

"Keeping the bugs occupied while you guys got out safely," Jensen replied.

"You left him alone?! Moogz, you know his machine isn't air-worthy!"

"Sorry, Cap, but he ordered me to help you two. And I ain't about to go against the chain of command. Not after what he pulled. Don't worry. We both know he can take care of himself. Ready?"

Altair sped through clouds, following the sounds of explosions and rapid gunfire, to return to where Jensen had left Owen. The mist had cleared up and they saw that Fenrir had met up with the others on the islands and continued their attack on the Goliath class bugs. Minotaur was blasting away with its dual gatling guns to get two hornets in the right position before launching a couple of missiles from the pods on its waist. The missiles reached their targets and obliterated them from the sky. Fenrir and Kirin skated along the strip of land, distracting and trying to corner the horned-beetle while Agni prepared a couple of charges to slap on it. The beetle reacted before Agni could make contact and kicked the machine into the water.

The four other hornets swooped in, launching acid-tipped stingers at Fenrir and Kirin. One of the stingers broke through Kirin's left elbow and melted the joint off. The hornet's head blew off in a shower of blood and goo before it could attack again. Gryphon landed beside Kirin, sniper rifle at the ready, and shot at another hornet. Altair transformed and landed next to the two.

Fenrir continued its attack on the beetle, not letting up or giving it time to attack. Owen saw an opening from above and jumped. Fenrir drew out its sword, but the beetle opened up its shell and whacked the mech out of the air. Fenrir landed on the rocky sides of the island, systems overheating. The beetle jumped on top of it, pinning Fenrir to the ground, and repeatedly bashed it with its horn, tearing off pieces of the outer frame.

A bomb exploded on the beetle's shell. It let out a loud shriek twisted with pain and anger. Agni stood behind the bug, water dripping from its parts, tossing a bomb up and down like a baseball. "Batter up!" Mark called out and threw the bomb at the beetle. The beetle's shell blew off and exposed its membranous wings. It took off into the air and launched plasma bolts at Agni. Mark evaded the bolts, only to get ambushed by one of the hornets. The new enemy tore off Agni's head as it zoomed through the air.

Minotaur sprayed bullets, trying to shoot the bugs out of the sky while Kirin took more precise shots with its rifle. Gryphon set up its sniper rifle behind the other two A.R.M.s, and tried to line up a shot as quickly as possible. Altair got caught in a dogfight with the beetle while the other two hornets tried to pry off Agni's outer armor. Fenrir hadn't moved since.

"Any time now, Cap!" Chase cried as the last of his missiles missed their target.

"Shut up and keep up with the cover fire!" Ephraim ordered.

"Ammunition running low!" T.N. informed.

"I know!" Ephraim shouted. *Come on! Come on!*

"Just breathe, Cap," Casey said, placing her hand on his shoulder.

Ephraim took a deep breath and squeezed the trigger on his exhale. The bullet whizzed by Minotaur and Kirin, and ripped through the hornet's body, sending it crashing into the ocean depths.

"Eat that, mother fucker!" Chase roared.

"It's too early to be celebrating!" Ephraim said. "T.N., see to Ghost! Merc, blast those bugs off of Boom!"

"Roger!" both soldiers responded.

Minotaur aimed its shoulder Vulcans at the two hornets and opened fire. The bullets weren't strong enough to do any real damage, but it was enough to get the bugs' attention off of Agni and on Minotaur. The hornets let out angry shrieks and chitters just before they rushed Minotaur at high speed. Chase smiled as Minotaur emptied its Gatling guns on the bugs. Nothing was left of them when the guns clicked empty.

"Ghost! Ghost, do you read?" T.N. shouted when Kirin reached Fenrir. "Owen!"

Inside Fenrir's cockpit, Owen frantically tried every boot-up procedure to reactivate the A.R.M. "Come on, Fenrir!" he growled. "Wake up!" he screamed, slamming his fist on the main console. The machine's instruments lit up and the systems reactivated. "Yes!"

"Owen!" T.N. called through the now-functioning radio. "You alive in there?"

"No way in hell am I going to die in this retarded-ass battle!" Owen roared.

Fenrir sprang to life and blasted off into the air. Burning its thrusters at full, Fenrir blazed passed Altair and straight into the beetle. The bug shot a large plasma bolt that blew off Fenrir's left leg, but Owen powered on through. Fenrir raised its sword and plunged it into the beetle's exposed back. The shrill squeal of pain echoed throughout the islands as Fenrir repeatedly stabbed the bug.

"Boom! Moogz!" Owen shouted.

"Roger!" Agni tossed one of its bombs to Fenrir to stick it in the open wound. Fenrir jumped off the bug just as Altair released a missile barrage, setting off the bomb. The combined explosions sent bits of beetle splattering all over the islands and A.R.M.s. The smoke cleared and the echoes of gunfire faded.

The battle was finally over.

Altair transformed and landed on the largest of the islands to join the others. All six pilots got out of their machines, breathing heavily. Ephraim helped Casey to the ground.

"Man, that was a bitch of a battle!" Mark groaned, stretching and cracking his back.

"Yeah," Jensen agreed. He looked at all the A.R.M.s and the remains of Fat Boy. Half the machines were heavily damaged, and they were all extremely low on ammunition. "We've seen better days."

"They were following us," Owen muttered, leaning against Fenrir's good leg.

Ephraim stomped over to Owen and slammed him against his

mech. "What the hell were you thinking, Lieutenant?!" he barked. "Where do you get the nerve to challenge my authority?"

"Cap, take it easy," Jensen said, going up to them, but was stopped by Chase.

"Let them fight it out," he said. "They need it."

"Well?" Ephraim demanded.

"I'm sorry, *Captain*," Owen began, keeping his tone neutral, but overemphasizing Ephraim's rank, "but I didn't know I needed orders to save our lives."

"You call this saving our lives?!" Ephraim pointed to their units as he spoke, taking in the extensive damage they suffered. "We're in the middle of god-knows where because of you! Jensen could have distracted the bugs long enough for the rest of us to recover and prepare for a counterattack!"

"We're alive, aren't we?" Owen stated without remorse. "Besides, fearless leader, why—no. Never mind."

"You have something to say to me, then say it!"

"No." Owen pushed Ephraim off of him, turning to walk away. "I did the right thing. I don't regret my actions."

"Say it!" Ephraim demanded.

Owen turned back around and spat, "As our leader it should have been you to be the first one out, not me! Rather than spending so much time following procedure and awaiting orders, you need to start taking more action, unless you want everyone to die from your lack of trust in your instincts."

Owen's cool composure came back just as quickly as he had lost it. "This is your family you wish to protect," he said bitterly. "Not mine."

With those last words, Ephraim lost it and punched Owen in the face. Owen was caught off guard by the sudden strike and fell to the sand. "If you feel that way, then why are you here?" Ephraim breathed heavily, restraining his anger to keep from lashing out even more.

Owen didn't make any effort to recover.

"You may not care about us," Ephraim continued, "but we care about you, goddammit! Your lone-wolf shit isn't gonna fly in this unit." He took a breath and let it out slowly. "I get that you lost your family. I do. But you're not the only who has lost someone. And that is no excuse for disobeying orders and acting on your own," he continued. "We are a team, Lieutenant, and your family now. Whether you like it or not is your problem, but that's how it is and will be. And if you ever disobey my orders again, I will have you stripped of your rank and machine, and if need be, I'll personally throw you back into the wilderness where we found you." He then turned and walked away.

Mark went over to Owen and helped him up. "You all right, buddy?" he asked.

"I've been through worse," Owen replied.

"Was that really necessary, Cap?" Jensen asked as Ephraim walked by him. "That threat, I mean."

"How far away are we from our destination, T.N.?" Ephraim asked, ignoring Jensen.

"Judging from satellite positioning," T.N. said, typing away at his terminal, "we are about 80 kilometers west off the coast of Great Britain. If our machine's cores were at capacity, we could use the A.R.M.s to travel the distance."

"But they're not, right?"

"Nope."

"Altair's is," Jensen said. Everyone looked at him. "Guys, you do remember that my mech's core has a larger power supply, right? It has twice the energy as the standard mech. I can fly over and bring back some help."

"Do it," Ephraim said.

"I need some weapons, just in case. My machine gun is out, and my rifle only has half a mag left."

"Take one of Gryphon's pistols and Kirin's rifle," Ephraim suggested. "That should be enough."

"Roger."

After Altair was prepped, Jensen headed out to bring back assistance. No one had said anything since he left. Chase fell asleep on a patch of grass. Mark made a makeshift fishing rod out of some detonator cord and a bug's antenna, and spent the time trying to catch a fish. T.N. was meditating in front of Kirin. Casey sat on a rock, quietly mourning her destroyed craft as it slowly sank into the ocean depths. Ephraim sat on the grass beside her, typing up his report on his terminal. Owen sat in Fenrir's cockpit, keeping an eye out for any more bugs.

No one said a word.

EPISODE 8: UNTESTED THEORY

19:44:21

"Man, that was tense!" Jensen said to himself, switching the Altair to silent run and activating the autopilot. "Glad to be away from that." While on silent run, Altair's heat signature was almost invisible to the Infestation's vision, but its speed was drastically reduced. It would take Jensen an hour to clear the distance to reach the mainland.

Jensen opened up his backpack and took out some canned meat to eat. It had been a really long day, and the events were taking a toll on him. *Man, why am I even here?* Jensen thought to himself. *My mom and dad are alive and happy. It wasn't our fault that we were picked to live in Arcadia before all of this shit. We were just lucky.* He took a swig of water from his canteen to wash down the canned meat and continued his musings.

The general called it survivor's guilt, and I guess it's true. I'm the only one in the team who hasn't lost anybody. That's the reason why I joined; to keep people from losing anybody again. Or so I say. Truth is I have no reason to fight. I shouldn't be here.

Everyone has a reason to fight, Jensen remembered Ephraim once say and his conversation with Chase. *And that reason is to survive.*

"Fight to survive, huh?" Jensen smiled. "Yeah, I can do that. As that saying goes, better to die on your feet than on your knees.

Thanks, bro." He said, finally reaching the mainland.

* * *

20:57:42

"This is Crusader A.R.M.s unit CRSD-03, Altair of Arcadia. Second Lieutenant Jensen Ford requesting permission to land."

"Roger that, CRSD-03," confirmed a female operator with a British accent. "You are cleared to land on runway 5. Welcome to Camelot."

"Copy that."

Camelot was a heavily fortified and rebuilt castle previously known as Conwy Castle, located in the northern coast of Wales. The castle looked over a small walled town. There were 22 guard towers along the quarter mile long wall. Altair landed in mech mode among other jets and mass-produced A.R.M.s, and Jensen lowered himself from the cockpit to the tarmac via pulley. He was greeted by the surrounding soldiers and was approached by a high-ranking officer.

"Colonel Wesley Grant," he introduced himself.

"Second Lieutenant Jensen Ford of the Crusader A.R.M.s, sir!" Jensen saluted.

"General Faulkner told me you were coming, but I was informed that a larger team would arrive."

"We ran into some trouble on the way here," he explained. "Our transport was shot down, and our machines are heavily damaged. My unit was the only one in condition enough to make the journey here."

"I see. Where are your mates now?" Colonel Grant asked.

"Stranded on a cluster of small islands about 80 kilometers east of here."

"Very well," said the colonel. "I'll send out a carrier to pick them up. You and your team can stay here and rest while your units are repaired."

"Thank you, sir." Jensen saluted and was dismissed.

* * *

21:29:11

Chase's loud snoring broke the silence. For almost two hours no one had said a word. After Ephraim's altercation with Owen, the others didn't want to risk saying anything that would set off either one. The moon hung low above the horizon, and the waves crashed gently against the rocks. Mark had given up on fishing and just sat in his mech's cockpit, chewing on a matchstick.

"I have to take a shit," he blurted.

"Hold it in," T.N. said from his meditation spot.

Fenrir suddenly activated, eyes glowing green, and righted itself on its good knee. It aimed the rifle at the area behind the group. "Incoming!" Owen announced through the radio.

Mark, Ephraim, and T.N. ran inside their A.R.M.s and took out their weapons, posting themselves behind their machines for cover. "Stay inside the cockpit, Casey," Ephraim ordered her. "Merc! Armor up!"

Chase snorted himself awake. "Fuck, man! I was dreaming about an endless bowl of rice!" He noticed everyone armed and in position, and then ran to his machine and armed himself.

The Crusaders held their positions, fingers twitching over the triggers. Fenrir's radio buzzed and a voice said, "Ease up on the weapons, guys. This is the carrier ship Avalon, our ride."

Owen relaxed a little and responded. "Copy that, Jensen. I confirm your presence."

"You better damned well confirm my presence," Jensen said.

A large battleship sailed out of the darkness and came to a stop 50 meters from the island. Its tender headed towards the mainland. "Board your A.R.M.s in the containers," he said after saluting to Ephraim and the others. "The captain and your comrade will be waiting for you on the bridge."

"Understood," said Ephraim. "Time to go," he called out to the team.

"Thank god!" Chase bellowed. "I hope they have rice on there."

"I still need to take a shit," Mark said. Ephraim and T.N. rolled their eyes at him.

With the A.R.M.s onboard, the team met up with Jensen and the captain of the Avalon, Captain Arthur Smith, on the bridge. "I appreciate the help, Captain Smith," Ephraim said, saluting him.

"Any time, Captain Herrera. Your second lieutenant here informed us of what happened. Seems like you and your team had one hell of a battle."

"Yeah, we did. Is it okay if my team and I were to rest in the cabins?"

"By all means," Captain Smith nodded. "How do you say, *mi casa es su casa*," the British man said. That made Ephraim smile.

A sailor led them down the narrow corridors to the cabins. "The mess deck is down this corridor and the second right," he said. "Help yourselves."

"Thank you, sailor," Ephraim saluted. He turned to his team and said, "Get some food and rest, Crusaders. We'll reach Camelot in a couple of hours. And I guess we'll be stuck there for a few days."

"You don't have to tell me twice," Chase said, running to the kitchen. Mark and Jensen followed closely behind. The rest of the team entered one of the vacant cabins, and Casey plopped herself on the nearest bottom bunk.

"How you holding up, Case?" Ephraim asked.

"I'll be much better once I get back in the air," she moaned, face turning slightly green. Casey laid down on the bed and hugged a pillow to try and comfort herself.

"Owen?" Ephraim asked, but he was already asleep. "Okay. I'm gonna get some food. Toshi? Casey? You guys want anything?"

Casey moaned a decline, turning away from the door to face the wall.

"I'm fine," T.N. said. "Thanks."

Ephraim turned to Owen again, then left for the mess deck.

T.N. sat on the bunk above Casey, looking through his notes on his terminal. "He's gone now," he said, not turning away from his notes.

"So?" Owen mumbled.

"You can't avoid him forever."

"I'm not avoiding him," Owen said. "I'm exhausted."

"You may not agree with his methods, but he is our commanding officer for a reason. Whether you like it or not, Owen, Ephraim deserves your respect."

"Uh-huh," Owen mumbled.

T.N. continued to scroll through his notes in silence for a few minutes until he finally spoke. "Owen, you said something back on the island that piqued my curiosity."

"Something always piques your curiosity," Owen mumbled.

"True," he said after taking a moment to think upon Owen's words. "You said that the Infestation followed us. What did you mean by that?"

"It means what I said."

"Care to elaborate?"

"I care to sleep," Owen snarked back.

T.N. didn't say anything. For the next five minutes the only sounds that echoed in the room were Casey's seasick moans and the crashing of the waves.

Owen suddenly sat up, an annoyed scowl on his face. T.N. smiled. "In the five years Francis and I hunted them, the Infestation had never sent a hunting party after us. Granted we never stayed in the same place for too long to find out if they did send one after us."

"Meaning?" T.N. prodded.

"Meaning that the bugs simply seemed like normal insects that acted on instincts. Food. Shelter. Mating. Plain old bugs rather than an alien race."

"What if that's exactly what they are?" T.N. suggested.

"What do you mean?"

"What if the Infestation aren't aliens at all? What if they are just simple bugs?"

Owen pondered on the notion for a moment, recalling all of his past experiences with them. "That could explain their behavior in the past," he finally said. "But not their size or current behavior."

"I don't know about their current behavior, but I might have a theory for their size."

Owen arched an eyebrow. "Withholding information on us, Toshi? That's not like you."

"Speaking this much this long without brushing me off is unlike you, Owen," T.N. smiled. "Dr. Noble must really be getting through to you."

"Your theory?" Owen urged with annoyance lacing his voice.

T.N. jumped down from his bunk and sat next to Owen. "Take a look at this," he said, handing the lieutenant his terminal.

"What am I looking at?" Owen asked, taking the terminal.

"An x-ray of the Type-2 we captured this morning. Notice

anything odd?"

Owen scrutinized the image more closely. His eyes bulged open when he noticed the oddity. "It has an endoskeleton! Wait. I thought insects only had an exoskeleton."

"They do," T.N. confirmed. He changed the image to one of the Worker's internals. "And take a look at the organ formation."

"So what? How does this justify them not being aliens? For all we know, this could be just their physiology."

T.N. hesitated for a moment, but Owen glared at him, a look that T.N. and the others knew too well. That look said one of two things: drop the subject before it goes too far, or talk before Owen made them talk. T.N. gulped and said, "Back at the academy, before the storm, Professor Kirchner was developing a serum that would kick-start humanity's next evolutionary step to better prepare for long journeys into space."

Oh...kay?"

"You know that extended periods in zero gravity deteriorates the bones, right?"

"Yeah, so?"

"Scientists believed that insects are better suited for zero-G environments than on Earth. Something about the weightlessness allowing them to grow bigger and stronger."

"Still not proving your point, T."

"Before the storm, a geneticist by the name of William Matthias stole the formula and modified it to aid in his DNA splicing projects. He injected himself with it after killing Kirchner in front of me, and I saw him start to change, but the ceiling caved in before I got a good look. Kirchner's last words to me were to fight for survival." T.N. took a breath and let it out slowly. "The meteors struck soon after, bringing with them the Infestation. Or so we're led to believe."

"So you're saying that this Matthias guy may be the reason for all the giant bugs?" Owen asked, trying to follow his comrade's train of thought.

"The original purpose for Kirchner's formula was to accelerate humanity's evolution to become stronger, faster, and have better endurance in zero-G environments, all while having a flexible bone structure. Matthias wanted to create an army of super soldiers and saw the formula as the missing link."

"So he used the formula, along with his super soldier theories to create what? Human-insect hybrids? That's what you're trying to say?" Owen saw T.N. nod slowly. "That could explain the sudden rise in their strategy. Have you mentioned this to Ephraim or General Faulkner?"

T.N. shook his head. "It's all still speculation with barely any evidence. I need more substantial proof before I confirm anything and tell the others."

"Tell the others what?" Mark asked as he, Chase, Jensen, and Ephraim reentered the room.

The cabin was painted tan and had a grey tiled floor. There were three bunk beds in the room, one against each wall. Chase laid down on the bottom bunk facing the door. Ephraim climbed up on the top bunk. Mark climbed up on the bunk above Owen's, feet hanging off the edge. Jensen sat on the bunk where Casey was resting, careful not to disturb her. T.N. returned to his top bunk on the right side of the room.

"What were you guys talking about?" Ephraim asked.

Owen looked at T.N., who let out a reluctant sigh. He spent the next few minutes explaining his theory to the others. They listened intently as T.N. spoke. They knew that when he had a theory he wanted to prove, T.N. would follow it through until he got every piece of evidence to prove it. Whether he was right or wrong didn't matter to him, so long as he got the truth.

However, T.N. was usually correct about his theories, and the others grasped the horrible possibility that a single madman could be responsible for the near eradication of the human race. They also realized that, if T.N. was right, this William Matthias was responsible for the deaths of their loved ones and their tragic pasts. Owen fought to restrain his anger.

EPISODE 9: WEAPON PACKS

October 6, 2199

17:23:45

Upon arrival at Camelot, Ephraim contacted General Faulkner and gave him a report about their situation. However, he left out the details of Owen's insubordination and T.N.'s theory upon T.N.'s request. Despite the extent of the damage, the Crusaders' A.R.M.s were completely repaired in less than a week. T.N. and Chase joined the engineers to equip the new weapons packs on the six machines.

The Altair received a booster pack that increased its speed and maneuverability in both modes. The pack also came with a supply of 50 extra missiles and two pairs of high caliber machine guns, both of which could be used in either mode. The pack also supplied the Altair with extra fuel for longer flights.

Agni was upgraded with thicker shoulder and chest armor. The shoulder armor could be attached to the hands with extendable claws to better utilize Mark's brawling abilities. Agni's legs were also outfitted with thrusters to increase its land agility and air stability. It was also given a pair of high-powered shotguns to round out its firing capabilities.

Minotaur, already highly modified with thicker armor and modular weapon options, received a pair of deployable treads on its feet for increased ground mobility. Its verniers were upgraded to compensate for the added weight.

Kirin's shoulder armor was modified to incorporate a prototype sensor array that is able to calculate the position of surrounding enemies and send the data to the advanced computer T.N. had built for his machine. Along with the shoulder sensors, Kirin received a staff with retractable superheated blades on the ends. The staff could also be split in two to be used as escrima sticks to better suit T.N.'s fighting style.

Gryphon received a camouflage cloak that absorbs the mech's heat signature, making it almost invisible to the Infestation's vision. It also gained a compact version of the Eagle Eye high-powered sniper rifle, making it the first portable plasma-based weapon. The rifle was also capable of producing a short plasma blade from the barrel capable of cutting through steel. Gryphon was equipped with an energy backpack to give the Eagle Eye a steady supply of energy for large blast-radius shots.

Fenrir's verniers were upgraded to increase its already tremendous speed. It was also outfitted with a pair of deployable wings to give it much better aerial mobility. The katana was replaced with a saber-like weapon for single-hand use. The weapon came equipped with a superheated blade to allow Fenrir to slice through the Infestation's thick shells with greater ease. A pair of four-barreled mini Gatling guns were installed on the mech's clavicle to give it much better mid-range capabilities.

"We're all repaired and ready to go, General," Ephraim said, talking to General Faulkner through the video link. Ephraim noticed the look of concern on his face. "Did something happen, General?"

"The Titans have not checked-in in three days," he said. "In their last transmission, they reported a series of caverns underneath the Oval Office and went to investigate."

"Did you want us to go and look for them, sir. It'll give us a chance to test out our new equipment."

"No. Return straight to Arcadia. No detours. It's been too quiet these past couple of days. I don't like it. I repeat, Captain Herrera: back to base."

"Yes, sir." Ephraim saluted and cut the feed. He joined the others in the hanger, careful to avoid the personnel carts that were zipping by. The hanger was approximately a mile in length, and housed an assortment of A.R.M.s and other military vehicles.

"What did he say?" Jensen asked, sitting on the foot of Altair. "Did he ask about me?"

"He said to come straight home. Also that the Titans haven't sent in their report in three days."

"Wait, the Titans are missing?" Mark asked, dropping the matchstick he had in his mouth.

"Not missing," Ephraim clarified. "Just haven't checked in. Faulkner said that they found some caverns under the Oval Office, of all places."

"And the general doesn't want us to investigate?" T.N. asked.

Ephraim shook his head. He looked around and then asked, "Where's Casey?"

A loud scream rang from the far end of the hanger. Ephraim and the others ran from their A.R.M.s to the source of the scream. When they reached it, they saw Casey in tears, hugging the wheel of a large transport ship. The wheel was bigger than her.

"Casey, what's wrong?" Ephraim asked, afraid she was being attacked.

"He's alive!" she cried. "He's alive! He's alive! He's alive!"

The guys looked from her to the craft and immediately recognized it. Fat Boy had been resurrected. "So that means we can pack up and go home now?" Mark asked.

"How did Fat Boy get here?" Ephraim asked.

"My team salvaged the wreckage and brought it back here," Colonel Grant answered as he approached the team. "We repaired it and gave it a heat-absorbing coat of paint. It shouldn't draw as much attention from the Infestation as before. We've also upgraded its engines and installed a drone to provide aerial support, along with auto-turrets capable of firing sabot incendiary rounds."

Casey ran up to Colonel Grant and gave him the biggest hug she could manage. "Thank you! Thank you! Thank you!" she repeated, kissing him on the cheek.

"It was no problem at all, miss," he chuckled. "That ship is a fine piece of machinery. It would be a shame to let it rust away in the ocean."

"He's my fat boy," she said. Both stood in silence, admiring the gigantic plane.

"Aw, how cute," Ephraim cooed. "Casey and the colonel are

having a moment."

Mark, Jensen, and Chase did a simultaneous "Aw!" and Casey's face turned redder than a tomato, but Colonel Grant laughed.

"It's good to see you young soldiers can still have fun, even during these dark times," Grant said.

"Thank you for all of your help, Colonel," Ephraim said. "It's time for us to go. My fiancé will kill me if I don't return home."

"Godspeed, gentlemen," Grant saluted. "Ma'am."

The Crusaders saluted and prepared to make the journey back home.

*   *   *

19:55:13

Night had fallen and Fat Boy was halfway home. Ephraim sat in the copilot seat next to Casey while the others sat with their A.R.M.s. The convoy shipping the weapon packs for the other teams followed close behind. T.N. was checking the A.R.M.s systems for any irregularities in the programming updates. Mark sat in Agni's cockpit, studying the operations manual. Jensen and Chase sat on the ground, playing cards. Owen sat inside Fenrir, keeping an ever-watchful eye on the sensors for the enemy.

"All finished," T.N. said.

"With what?" Jensen asked, not looking away from his cards.

"You finished updating the OS to all six machines?" Chase asked.

T.N. nodded. "All that's left is for each of you to make your personal calibrations on the system."

"Awesome!" Mark cheered. He dropped the manual and started calibrating Agni's systems. Owen did the same with Fenrir.

"Cap," T.N. called on the radio. "Gryphon is set. Come down and do your thing."

"Got it," Ephraim responded. He joined the others down in the cargo hold and started working on his calibrations. Suddenly, his terminal beeped with a sense of dread. He grabbed it from the holster and opened it up. "Herrera," he answered.

"Get your asses back here on the double!" General Faulkner ordered, alarm and urgency in his voice.

"What's wrong, General?" he asked, unease creeping in.

"Full frontal assault!" Faulkner shouted before the transmission was cut off.

"Shit!" Ephraim seethed. "Casey!"

"On it!" she responded through the radio, and put Fat Boy on full burn.

EPISODE 10: NIGHT RAID

20:53:22

A dozen Drakes, Armored Scarabs, Type-2 workers, and Goliath-class hornets swarmed around Arcadia. The scarabs dropped the workers into the city like bombs, except the explosions came from the A.R.M.s that defended their city. A hail of cannon fire roared from the city's automated defenses. It looked like fireworks coming from outside the city.

"Shoot those damn things out of the sky before they drop more!" General Faulkner ordered the aerial team. He led the ground forces in his custom A.R.M. made to look like a white knight with a billowing blue cape. He called it Excalibur, and it held on its left hand a large white shield with a gold cross on it, and wielded an equally impressive broadsword. Its edges were red-hot as it sliced through mantis after mantis.

The aerial team swooped and sped around the buzzing bugs, trying to keep anymore from reaching the city. Captain Joseph Wilson and his Jason A.R.M. led the team once again, but with the Titans missing and the Crusaders making their way back, the formation was severely hindered. "All right, team," he announced. "We are two units short, so our usual maneuvers won't work. Assume Gatling formation!"

The four flight units flew high into the moonlight. Some of the bugs watched as the A.R.M.s came down in mech mode, spinning back-to-back and shooting their rifles at the Infestation. The rest of the flying bugs swarmed in for the attack, but were ripped apart by the A.R.M.s' bullets. The bugs let out loud shrieks of pain, signaling for reinforcements. Three Goliath-class horned-beetles flew into the fray, their massive wings beating the air like the blades of helicopters. They released a volley of plasma bolts at the machines, breaking their formation. The A.R.M.s turned back into fighter mode and scattered.

On the ground, Faulkner charged into battle, slicing and stabbing the mantises with ease. Excalibur's cape spread like azure wings as it moved around the buildings and streets. The other 20 units backed Faulkner up with missile assaults and bullet sprays. One particular team, called Berserkers, rushed in beside him and attacked the surrounding enemy in a savage fury, staying true to their name. Excalibur and the five Berserkers held their ground as the next wave made their way to them.

"Where are you boys?" Faulkner said to himself.

*   *   *

22:03:42

Arcadia was finally within view when the Crusaders deployed out of Fat Boy. The carrier ship and the weapons transport continued toward the city. With their new weapons packs, the Crusaders were able to maintain aerial mobility without stressing their thrusters.

"Moogz, join up with the rest of the air squad," Ephraim ordered. "The rest of us will head straight toward the city."

"You don't have to tell me twice," Owen said and accelerated past his team.

"Ghost, don't rush ahead!" Ephraim shouted.

The proximity sensors went off in all six mechs, forcing them to stop their advance. The machines looked around, glowing green eyes scanning nothing but darkness.

"Where is it?" Mark asked, finger twitching over the triggers.

Using Kirin's new sensor array, T.N. scanned their surroundings for any signs of the enemy. "Above us!" he shouted.

A large plasma bolt shot down toward them, but the Crusaders evaded it just in time. Minotaur aimed its gatling guns in the air and let them rip, hoping to hit whatever attacked them. Nothing. T.N. scanned again. Nothing.

Owen listened intently, searching for any telltale signs. Then he heard it, a faint buzzing. He looked at his radar and saw faint blips moving rapidly towards them. "Incoming!"

The Crusaders readied their weapons as the lights grew brighter and the buzzing louder. The lights flickered a bit before becoming intensely bright again. "Evasive maneuvers!" Ephraim ordered.

Beams of pure energy blazed across the sky as the incoming firefly types fired them from their abdomens. There were three dozen of them, all roughly six meters long. Their brown-colored bodies made them difficult to see in the dark. The only real warning the Crusaders got were the abdomens' light right before their attack.

"Incredible!" T.N. gasped. "A new breed of bugs with bio-electric generation. I must procure one!"

"We're not procuring anything, T.N.," Owen growled. "They're going to die. They are all going to die!" Fenrir let out a barrage of bullets to scatter the fireflies, then zipped towards the closest one and sliced its head off. Fenrir flew away before the other bugs could shoot their energy beams at it. "I'll lead them toward land!" Owen radioed as Fenrir flew to the barren land ahead. "You guys take out as many as you can!"

"There he goes again," Ephraim grumbled. "Giving me orders."

"It's not a bad plan, though, Cap," Jensen said. Altair flew towards the fireflies chasing Fenrir, shooting at them with its machine guns.

Minotaur joined Altair and both launched a pair of scatter missiles, taking out three of the highly agile fireflies and breaking the formation of the others. Agni shot a grenade into the regrouping bugs, taking out two more. The fireflies diverted their attention from Fenrir to the others and rushed towards them.

Owen noticed, turned Fenrir around, and fired its rifle at them, but only two broke away from the others to pursue it. Kirin dropped in amongst the swarm, bladed staff in hand, and started cutting off heads and wings with expert precision as the staff twirled and spun around the machine. Gryphon flew past the others and the bugs to join Fenrir's side.

"What's your plan?" Ephraim asked through the radio as he

shot down three fireflies with one sweep of his rifle.

"We've got to get you set up with the Eagle Eye," Owen responded, slicing a bug in half. "We also have to get back to the city a.s.a.p.!"

"That last part's a given!" Ephraim grunted as Gryphon stabbed one of its knives in a firefly's eye.

The two mechs landed on the scorched earth and Gryphon got its sniper rifle ready. Agni and Minotaur joined Fenrir and formed a defensive line to protect Gryphon. Kirin and Altair stayed in the air to keep the bugs occupied. Minotaur launched more scatter missiles in the air, taking out another five fireflies. Four of them aimed their abdomens at the grounded A.R.M.s, but Agni punched them out of the air before they could fire the beams.

Suddenly, a group of Type-2 workers crawled their way out from the ground and started surrounding the A.R.M.s, launching blast after blast of plasma. Fenrir blocked them with its shield, and charged into the creatures. "Any time, Cap!" Owen shouted as Fenrir used its superheated saber to slice through bug after bug.

"Eagle Eye charged!" Ephraim said. "Targeted and firing!" Gryphon squeezed the trigger on the rifle and released a large yellow beam of energy at the fireflies, disintegrating six of them.

Kirin and Altair had gotten out of the line of fire, but the beam was bright enough to light up the night sky and temporarily blind their cameras.

"Holy fuck!" Mark gasped. "I want one!" Agni punched a worker in the face as the blades from the gauntlets tore off its head.

"Stay focused, Boom!" Ephraim ordered, shooting another beam at the remaining fireflies, sweeping it across the sky.

Proximity alarms blared again and Minotaur aimed its gatling guns toward the rocky hills behind it. Another large plasma bolt sped through the air. Minotaur evaded it, but it wasn't fast enough. Its left arm took the brunt of the blast and blew off. Three Goliath-class stag beetles dropped down from the sky and let out monstrous squeals. Their pinchers snapping open and closed as they rushed toward the damaged machine. Chase struggled to right Minotaur, but the blast knocked its stabilizers off balance.

The stag beetles were almost upon him, but in a flash of light, two of the beetles were cut into pieces, and a beam of energy reduced the third to ashes. Chase looked at his monitors and saw that Fenrir, Agni, and Kirin were standing in front of him. From the rear cameras, Chase saw Gryphon loading another energy cap into the Eagle Eye.

"Cutting it a little too close, aren't you guys?" Chase asked.

"I get it!" Mark chuckled.

"Is that the last of them?" Jensen asked as the Altair landed next to the others.

"I don't know," Ephraim said, leaving his perch to join his team. "Ghost, what do you see?"

Owen scanned the five large monitors that displayed his surroundings. He changed the spectrum from night vision, to infrared, to ultraviolet, and then back to normal. "Fenrir can't see anything around us," he reported.

"Then let's hurry back!" Mark urged. "The city needs us!"

"Merc, you functional?" Ephraim asked.

"Minotaur's had worse," Chase responded, finally getting his A.R.M. to stand.

"Good. Crusaders, move out!"

"Roger!" everyone responded.

Just then, the land started to rumble violently, tearing large fissures into the bedrock. The Crusaders took to the air and witnessed a monstrous centipede, at least 200 meters long, burrow its way out of the earth, shrieking and squealing as its mandibles snapped open and closed. Its many legs kicked furiously in the air as its antennae flailed about, smelling its surroundings. The sight of this new adversary terrified them all, especially Owen.

End Volume 1

The Crusaders will return in Volume II: Contingencies, available now in all online stores. And follow the adventures of the masked vigilante Nightmare as he prowls the streets of Silverstone City in the Scarred Nightmare Series, Book I: Fading Howl, and Book II: Fading Memories, also available in all online bookstores.

General's Log

Date: October 1, 2199

Entry: 1-001

Title: Arcadia

Seventy years ago the world finally came together to unite under a single banner. They proposed the Arcadia project, an artificial land roughly the size of Texas floating above the Pacific Ocean. This land took fifty years to complete, but it solidified the new world order, known as the New Earth Republic Alliance, or New E.R.A.

Arcadia is home to roughly 25 million people, with search parties going out into the wastelands in search of survivors of the Great Storm. The city is divided into five different sectors:

- The residential sector: self-explanatory. The citizens of Arcadia live in enormous buildings with apartment-like quarters.
- The industrial sector: filled with factories to produce clothing, supplies, and other materials we need to live comfortably.
- The natural sector: littered with trees, plants, wildlife, and several artificial waterfalls and lakes.
- The commercial sector: also known as the business district, it contains shopping centers, amusement parks, playgrounds, and other things people need to get their minds off the destruction outside the walls of Arcadia.

● The central hub: home to the red-light district, as well as the command tower that acts as headquarters to our fighting force, the six A.R.M.s teams, and the scores of fighter jets and tanks.

Arcadia is not the only human settlement in existence. Great Britain has the walled castle town dubbed Camelot, which supports 12 million people. China's former Shanghai is now known as Shangri-La, home to roughly 30 million people. Central and South America has El Dorado, holding a little over 40 million people. The African continent has Alexandria, sheltering 2.3 billion people.

Yeah. In a world that once populated 7 billion people, less than half survived the storm.

Entry: 1-002

Title: Storm

The completion of Arcadia occurred on February 1st, 2179. The celebration was lively and immense, but was cut short. Two weeks later planet Earth was ravaged by a freak meteor storm that decimated a quarter of the planet. But that wasn't the worst of it. This storm brought with it a race of savage insect-like aliens that hunted and slaughtered the human race. New E.R.A. calls these aliens the Infestation.

But something doesn't add up. Not to me. One would think that our astronomers would have seen these meteors coming, thus preventing the invasion.

Unless they weren't meteors...

If they weren't, then what were they? Missiles, maybe? Was it an attack by one of the nations that refused to join the New E.R.A.? Or was it merely the actions of a separate group with no affiliations to the sovereign nations? If so, then how did they get access to so much firepower?

Thinking about this raises so many questions. Unfortunately, the only ones with the answers, or at least access to, are the members of the Faculty, who reside in their floating fortress high in the clouds like a bunch of gods. I won't expect help from them.

Science Officer Nikaido is pursuing these same questions, too. I'm sure of it. But I fear that he might be spreading himself too thin with all of his responsibilities. I can't have that. I need him focused more on his team than anything else.

Entry: 1-003

Title: Infestation

These insect-like aliens have terrorized the Earth for two decades, and we've little information to show for it. We have several classifications for the Infestation, but other than that, we know nothing. I'm hoping S.O. Nikaido will be able to find some new information once he analyses the specimen he captured this morning.

From what we do know, the Infestation can be separated into different classes:

•Worker class – there are two types of the Worker class, Type-1 and Type-2. Type-1s are man-sized ant creatures with the strength to carry 50 times their weight. I've seen these things rip a man in half as if he were tissue paper. Type-2s are 12-meter tall creatures that look like a praying mantis that walk up on two legs and have four bladed arms. The reason why we group these two together despite their differences is because they are the most common types we've encountered over the years.

•Soldier class – these are 7-foot tall roaches that have excellent night vision, immense speed, and, just as the regular cockroach, can survive radiation and can live several weeks without its head. I've only encountered this class twice, both times when I was near the creatures' nest 15 years ago.

•Winged class – despite most classes of the Infestation having wings, this class is usually seen in the air more than on the ground, taking a more supportive role than the Workers or Soldiers. The Winged ones have two distinct subspecies. The Armored Scarabs act like the couriers by dropping cocoons filled with larvae, or other bugs into the city like bombs. The other subspecies is known as Drakes, dragonfly-type creatures capable of high-speed flights that rival our fastest flyers.

• Goliath class – as the name suggests, these are giant bugs, between 30 to 50 meters in length. So far we've only encountered two types, hornets able to shoot acidic stingers that can melt through an A.R.M.'s armor and fly at incredible speeds, and a rhinoceros beetle type, 50 meters in length, powerful wings under a protective shell, and a giant horn that can be used as a battering ram or bludgeoning weapon.

• Queen class – we've only encountered one queen within the 20 years of the fighting, but all of these bugs were born from that one bug. It is safe to assume that during the 15-year hibernation the Infestation went on, they likely bred a new queen to take over the one that was destroyed by a little boy and his older brother.

One common trait the Infestation has among all of its subspecies is that they are all capable of releasing plasma bolts through their mouths. These bolts contain enough concussive force to blast a hole through solid stone, but steel and other durable metals can withstand several of these blasts with some effort.

Entry: 1-004

Title: A.R.M.

Armored Response Mechs, the New E.R.A.'s most advanced fighting force of 15-meter tall humanoid robots operated by via a cockpit system located in the torso. Originally developed as a means to cross all forms of terrain during times of war, they were later decommissioned once the new world order was created. However, they were brought back into action as soon as the Infestation arrived.

Because they were decommissioned for over fifty years, there were originally only 75 A.R.M.s in action during the initial attack. We lost half that force back then. However, our scientists have developed a new generation of A.R.M.s, with help from a young genius by the name of Toshi Gin Nikaido. These 36 units have been separated into six teams of six, each bearing their own emblem and all piloted by the new wave of soldiers we've trained for fifteen years.

These teams are:

- Argonauts – named after the Greek sailors of the legendary ship, *Argo*. Their emblem is that of a red trireme with a golden ram's head on its prow.

- Crusaders – designated as such for their goal to stop the Infestation and secure humanity's survival. Their emblem is that of a winged sword with the point down in front of a crescent moon.

- Marauders – given the name as they are able to easily go out into the open world and loot historical artifacts that survived the storm, and use their stealth to sneak past the Infestation. Their emblem is that of a torn Jolly Roger.

- Berserker – a group of melee fighters who seem to go into a trance-like fury during battle. Their emblem is that of a man wearing a bearskin.

- Amazons – an all female group. Fierce, agile, and just as strong as the others. Their tightly-knit bond has made them famous for their ambush tactics. Their emblem is that of a maiden armed with a longbow.

- Titans – the first team of A.R.M.s to be created. Strong but a bit reckless. Their emblem is that of a sickle.

These new A.R.M.s are separated into three classes: Sniper, Aerial, and General Purpose.

The Sniper class specializes in long-range support rather than melee combat. Normally equipped with assault rifles, linear rifles, sniper rifles, and an assortment of missiles to tackle the mission. Captain Ephraim A. Herrera of the Crusaders is our best sniper and is often equipped with the high-caliber sniper rifle dubbed Eagle Eye.

The Aerial class is transformable. Able to quickly transform from a fighter jet to a standard mech at a moment's notice. Captain Joseph Wilson of the Argonauts is our fastest flyer while Second Lieutenant Jensen M. Ford is our most skilled flyer, able to perform unthinkable feats in the air that allows him to evade attacks.

The General Purpose class is self-explanatory. Built with a modular design that allows the pilot to customize their machines to suit their needs. Warrant Officer Chase Mercer of the Crusaders took the modular system to a whole new level by designing and integrating heavier armor that holds missiles and Gatling guns within it.

However, even with all information and the weapons we possess, the New E.R.A. has yet to come close to eradicating this threat to the human race. Will we endure? Only time will tell.

End log

General Ian Ulysses Faulkner

ABOUT THE AUTHOR

Omarr S. Guerrero is an independently published author who is making his way towards public recognition. Born and raised in San Diego, Omarr turned to writing as a way to give the voices in his head an outlet or else they would have made him crazier than he already is.

Made in the USA
Las Vegas, NV
02 March 2021